MIRA AND THE STONE TORTOISE

Hoo Ga Ga Hoo Ga Ga Hoo Hoo Hoo!

For Frances and Sher Lilly
—M. L.

Mira and the Stone Tortoise is based on "The Tortoise Who Tricked the Man," from *Amazonian Tortoise Myths*, by Fred Hartt. Rio de Janeiro: William Scully, 1875.

This story is from the Kulina of Brazil.

ILLUSTRATIONS © Charles Reasoner

Library of Congress Cataloging-in-Publication Data

Lilly, Melinda.
  Mira and the stone tortoise / retold by Melinda Lilly;   illustrated by Charles Reasoner.
      p. cm.—(Latin American tales and myths)
  Summary: After befriending a clever tortoise while lost in the Brazilian rain forest, a young Kulina girl helps it keep from becoming her father's dinner.
  ISBN 1-57103-264-9
  1.Culina Indians—Folklore. 2. Tales—Amazon River Region.[1. Culina Indians—Folklore. 2. Indians of South America—Brazil—Folklore. 3. Folklore—Brazil.] I. Reasoner, Charles, ill. II. Title II. III. Series: Lilly, Melinda. Latin American tales and myths.
  F2520.1.C84L55 1999
  398.2'089'98081—dc21   98–12113
                                                                                    CIP
                                                                                    AC

Printed in the USA

Latin American Tales and Myths

MIRA
AND THE STONE TORTOISE

A Kulina Tale

Retold by
Melinda Lilly

Illustrated by
Charles Reasoner

The Rourke Press, Inc.
Vero Beach, Florida 32964

One afternoon, a young girl named Mira strolled behind her two older brothers as they walked through the rain forest on their way to catch fish. The beautiful day seemed to call to her and she meandered, skipping this way and that way on either side of the path. She slowed to admire a butterfly's shining wings as it fluttered nearby. She paused to touch the soft petals of an orchid blooming on a tree branch. She imitated the call of a howler monkey, "Hoo Ga Ga Hoo Ga Ga Hoo Hoo Hoo!" and tapped a beat on her basket. She fell farther and farther behind her purposeful brothers.

She heard a gravelly voice singing deep in the forest and stopped to listen.

I'm a howler monkey, just like you.
So bring me down a sapodilla fruit or two!
I'm a howler monkey, just like you.
So bring me down a sapodilla fruit or two!

The voice repeated the chant over and over.

Not thinking about her place at the end of the line or her brothers or fishing or anything but the scratchy voice, Mira left the trail. She hopped over muddy boulders, slippery *awa* tree roots, and a long line of *hani* leaf-cutter ants. She scooted over a log and came upon a *sapodilla* tree heavy with howler monkeys and fruit.

I'm a howler monkey, just like you.
So bring me down a sapodilla fruit or two!

The voice came from a small shrub right in front of Mira, at the bottom of the sapodilla tree. She bent over it, but saw only fat flappy leaves. The hidden voice loudly warned:

I can sing, howl, and hoot!
And I won't stop till I get some fruit!

"Hoo Ga Ga Hoo Ga Ga . . . stop singing!" shouted a howler monkey. Mira jumped out of the way just in time to avoid the shower of fruit. *Splat! Splat! Splat!* The wide leafy bush was covered in sapodilla goo.

Hoo Hoo Hoo!
We got you!

The monkeys laughed, bounding away through the treetops. Mira crept to the bush and slowly lifted one of its leaves. There, squatting under the shrub like a living fruit bowl, was a tortoise happily gobbling the mess.

"I knew you weren't a howler monkey!" Mira sang with triumph. "Now this is the sound of a howler monkey," she sang again, "Hoo Ga Ga Hoo Ga Ga Hoo Hoo Hoo!"

Tortoise shushed her and stopped chewing for a moment. "Sssshhhhh, I've got a good thing here, sssshhhhh!" He pulled off another bruised sapodilla and noisily chewed.

"Don't you know it's rude to eat alone?" asked Mira, plucking an unblemished fruit off Tortoise's back. "You don't seem to be rude," she added as she peeled it and took a big bite.

Chuckling with cheeks stuffed with sapodillas, Tortoise nodded his wrinkled head. "There's plenty, have some."

After both had eaten their fill, Mira looked up, trying to find the way back to the trail. The rain forest was darker now as afternoon deepened into evening. "I think I'm lost," Mira said. "And my family will be worried. They're probably looking for me now."

"I can help you find your way," offered Tortoise. "If you'll teach me to yell like a howler monkey."

"It's a deal," agreed Mira. "But it'll take practice!"

She lifted Tortoise onto her back and the two friends hooted and howled as Tortoise directed her back to the river. "Hoo Ga Ga Hoo Ga Ga Hoo Hoo Hoo!"

Soon they heard the voices of Mira's brothers calling as they looked for her, "Mira? Mira, where are you?"

Tortoise stopped singing and gave Mira a quick glance, saying, "Everybody's got to eat something, but I don't want to be anyone's dinner! Leave me here while you go back to your family." Mira gently set Tortoise under a bush.

"Thank you for guiding me," she whispered. "Will I see you again?

"Hoo Ga Ga! Perhaps," answered Tortoise with a grin.

Calling, "Hoo Ga Ga Hoo Ga Ga Hoo Hoo! Here I am!" Mira quickly met up with her brothers. "You won't believe it!" she enthused. "I met the most amazing—"

"Mira! We were so worried about you!" Ayo, her ten-year-old brother exclaimed. He hugged his little sister, scolding, "Don't you ever do that—!"

"We didn't get much time to fish because we were looking for you, Mira," interrupted Irano, the eldest. He tapped his fishing spear and bow on the ground. "I don't think Father is going to be too pleased with us around dinnertime."

"I'm sorry," she said, her eyes downcast.

"Sun's almost ready to sleep," said Ayo, leading the way down the trail. "Let's get going." To Mira, the walk back home seemed endless.

"You get to tell Father why we've only got two little fish, Mira," said Irano when they finally arrived at their hut.

Their father's happy voice greeted them, saying, "I found a special treat for our dinner tonight! My mouth is watering just thinking about it!"

Looking up at her father's grin, Mira sighed with relief. "We only caught two fish and it was my fault," she admitted.

He scooped her up in his arms and gave her a big kiss on the cheek. "That doesn't matter, Sweet Mira Mango." He laughed. "We'll have a wonderful dinner tonight! I found something delicious by the river."

He handed Irano a big, covered basket. "You mind the surprise for me while I pick some sapodilla fruits and collect wood for tonight's fire. Don't open the basket! I'll be back soon." Winking at his children, he headed off into the forest.

13

The children clustered around the basket, looking at it intently. It bumped! The children jumped back, then leaned in close. It scooted! The children followed it closely, eyes wide. A loud scratchy voice sang from inside the basket.

Hoo Ga Ga Hoo Ga Ga Hoo Hoo Hoo!
Hoo Ga Ga Hoo Ga Ga Hoo Hoo Hoo!

Mira gasped. It was the voice of Tortoise! Tortoise was the surprise dinner! "Let's open the basket and see what it is!" said Mira, thinking of her friend's predicament.

"We can't do that!" Irano reminded her sternly. "Father said not to!" He laid his arm across the top of the basket as Tortoise sang again.

Hoo Ga Ga Hoo Ga Ga Hoo Hoo Hoo!
Hoo Ga Ga Hoo Ga Ga Hoo Hoo Hoo!

"It's a howler monkey!" exclaimed Ayo. "Or a rooster, Co-co-ri-coo!" Tortoise answered.

> Hoo Ga Ga Hoo Ga Ga Hoo Hoo Hoo!
> No, no, no, that's not true!

Irano guessed, "It's a bird from the *babassu*?"

> Hoo Ga Ga Hoo Ga Ga Hoo Hoo Hoo!
> No, no, no, you're wrong too!

Tortoise sang. He hooted faster. Soon everyone was wiggling to a skip-tap, jump-slap, hop-clap howler monkey dancing tune.

Irano tried to look through the weave of the basket. He sang,

> Who? Who? Who? Wish I knew!

Tortoise sang.

> Hoo Ga Ga Hoo Ga Ga Hoo Hoo Hoo!
> Here's a clue what to do!
>
> Hoo Ga Ga Hoo Ga Ga Hoo Hoo Hoo!
> LET ME OUT, WHY DON'T YOU?

Irano flipped open the basket! Tortoise slid out, then spun on the floor! He bumped up on his hind legs and shimmy shimmied! He sang.

> Hoo Ga Ga Hoo Ga Ga Hoo Hoo Hoo!
> Dance with me! After you!

Tortoise followed the children dancing out the door. "Hoo Ga Ga Hoo Ga Ga Hoo Hoo Hoo!" everybody chanted. Jittering and skittering, they danced into the forest. Twirling and whirling, they danced on back! . . . Except one. Tortoise had slipped safely away to the forest.

"Where's Tortoise?" asked Irano, bringing the dancing line and the song to an abrupt stop. *Bump!* The children collided into each other.

Ayo stilled his tapping feet, glaring at them as though they'd betrayed him. "Oh, Father is going to be so mad and hungry too!"

Irano rubbed his forehead, trying to think. "Where could Tortoise have gone?"

"I know what we can do!" Mira whispered her plan to her brothers.

"All right," agreed Irano, reluctantly.

They quickly fanned out through the forest, searching under shrubs and along trails. They gathered black *pururiki* seeds, red fruit, and *tziba* rocks. They crushed the fruit and seeds for color and painted a flat rock until it looked just like a tortoise. Almost.

Mira set the rock tortoise into the basket and shut the lid. Then she and the others anxiously awaited their father's return.

Just as Sun was sliding below the tallest forest trees, Father arrived home whistling. He handed the sapodilla fruit to the children, stacked the wood, and sparked it into a campfire.

"Mmmm mmm, supper's soon and I can't wait!" he said, smacking his lips.

"Father, wouldn't you like to have fish tonight?" offered Irano, displaying the puny catch.

"You children can eat that if you want," Father smiled. "That'll leave more of the special dinner for me. Oh, I'm hungry for it, can almost taste it!" He skewered the fish and went inside the hut. Sun sank below the horizon and the sky dimmed.

Working slowly as it got darker, Mira peeled the skin off the sapodilla fruits in threads. Irano's arms barely moved as he ground the maize. Ayo kept getting in his father's way. Night overtook evening and the sky darkened almost to black.

"What's taking so long? You children hurry up, I'm hungry!" said Father, coming outside with the basket. He played with its latch, saying, "Irano, can you guess what it is? Should I give you a clue?"

"Howler monkey?" answered Irano, nervously.

"Howler monkey's fine, no doubt. But this is something else! Why, one bite and you'll shout for joy!"

"A bird?" mumbled Ayo, anxiously. "A rooster?"

"Rooster's tasty indeed, but nothing's as delicious as this," Father said with relish. He threw back the lid of the basket. "Just look at this tortoise, good and plump! Wait until you try it!" He lifted the rock tortoise out of the basket and dropped it into the fire. *Thunk!*

"Looks great, Father," Mira replied, trying to sound enthusiastic. As the family gathered around the campfire, clouds completely covered the sky and Moon hid below the Earth.

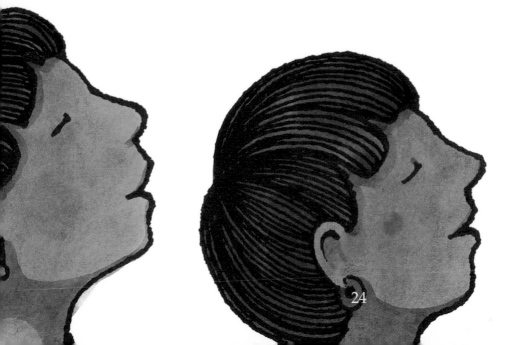

ather squinted into the flames. He rubbed his eyes, struggling to see. "That scales-and-bones fish is ready, I think," he said, pulling out the tiny catch. With great care he divided it into three parts and handed it to his children. "Think my dinner might be ready?" he wondered. "I'm more than ready to eat. There's nothing finer than a well-cooked tortoise."

"Better cook it a while longer," urged Mira.

"It must be cooked by now, but it doesn't smell ready," said Father, fanning the fire's smoke away from his face. "The last time I had it, I was about your age, Irano. I can still remember the sweet, smoky smell of the tortoise I ate that night." He breathed deeply and patted his belly.

"I can smell something," pretended Mira.

"Me too," agreed Irano, trying to keep the worry out of his voice. "Doesn't smell very good. Maybe you shouldn't eat it, Father."

Night wore on, at last becoming as dark as a tortoise's shell. "It's got to be almost charred by now," Father exclaimed. "And I'm hungrier than hungry!" He pulled the rock tortoise from the fire and tried to take a delicious bite with his wooden spoon. *Snap!* The spoon broke. Tossing it aside, he picked up the tortoise and bit hard. *Kkrrukk!* His tooth ground on the tough stone. "Ack!" he sputtered. "This is as hard as an old, dry fish!" Then he licked it. *Sllupp!* "Uggghh! It's awful!" he groaned. "The worst thing I've ever tasted!" In disgust, he threw the stone tortoise into the brush.

The children stifled their giggles and covered their grins with their hands.

"Whoever said we should eat tortoise?" Father went on, drinking a big jug of water to drown the bitter, dry taste. "I'm not eating this for a good, long time!" he exclaimed.

"Like forever?" offered Mira hopefully.

"At least until forever!" agreed Father.

"Here's some fish I saved for you, Father," said Mira gently, holding out her untouched dinner.

"Thank you, Mira, at least I won't go to bed hungry," he sighed.

After finishing their small meal, the family climbed into their hammocks to sleep. "I still can't believe I ever thought tortoise was tasty," Father grumbled as he rolled over. "Well, good night, all."

Smiling, the children answered "Good night, Father."

From somewhere in the forest, the children heard a distant voice singing under a sapodilla tree. The gravelly voice sounded just like a howler monkey. Almost.

Hoo Ga Ga Hoo Ga Ga Hoo Hoo Hoo!
Hoo Ga Ga Hoo Ga Ga Hoo Hoo Hoo!

PRONUNCIATION AND DEFINITION GUIDE

awa (AH wah) — Kulina for tree

Ayo (IY oh) — the name of a Brazilian boy

babassu (baw buh SOO) — a Brazilian palm.

hani (HAW nee) — Kulina for ant

Irano (ee RAH noh) — the name of a Brazilian boy

Kulina (koo LEE nah) — an Amazonian tribe that lives near the Jurua River in Brazil; the language of the Kulina people

mango (MANG goh) — a tropical tree and its fruit

Mira (MEE rah) — the name of a Brazilian girl

pururiki (poo roo REE kee) — Kulina for black

sapodilla (sap oh DIL ah) — a tropical tree with a sweet, brown-skinned fruit

tziba (TZEE bah) — Kulina for stone